A FILM BY TIM BURTON

A CINEMATIC STORYBOOK

ADAPTED BY
THOMAS MACRI

BASED ON THE SCREENPLAY BY
JOHN AUGUST

BASED ON AN ORIGINAL IDEA BY
TIM BURTON

Printed in the United States of America

First Edition

1 3 5 7 9 10 8 6 4 2

V381-8386-5-12197

ISBN 978-1-4231-8017-3

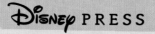

DISNEP PRESS

NEW YORK

SUSTAINABLE FORESTRY INITIATIVE

Certified Chain of Custody
At Least 20% Certified Forest Conte
www.sfiprogram.org
SFI-00993

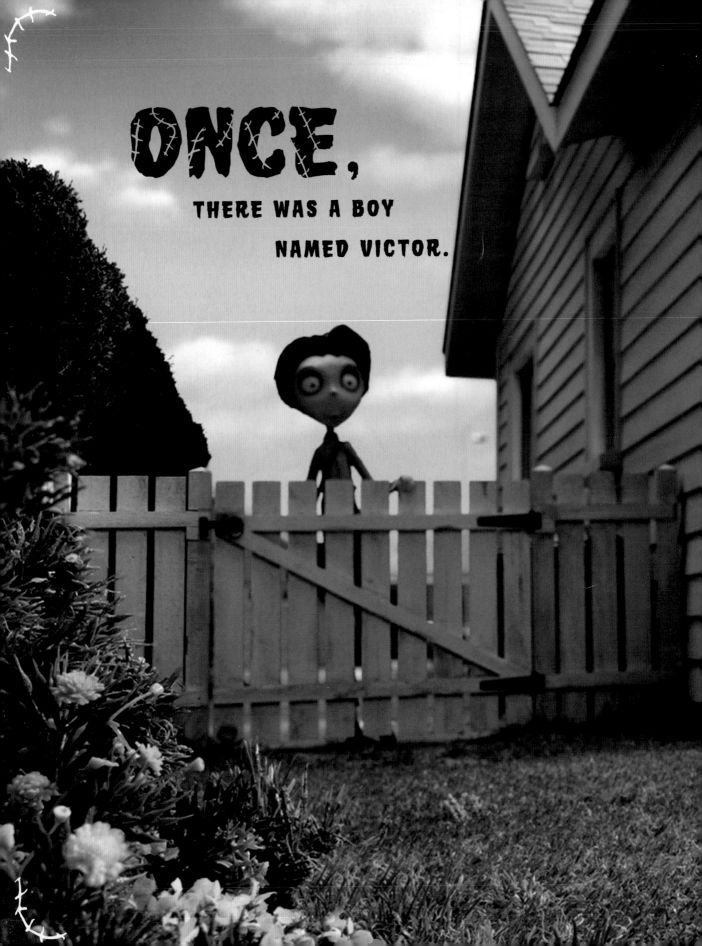

AND A DOG NAMED SPARKY.

AND
SPARKY
LOVED VICTOR.

AND

TOGETHER THEY PLAYED . . .

AND
MADE MOVIES.

SOMETIMES

IN 3-D!

SPARKY

WAS ALWAYS THE STAR.

ONE DAY,
WHILE VICTOR WAS
PLAYING BASEBALL,

WHICH WAS NOT SOMETHING
HE LOVED TO DO,

HE SWUNG HIS BAT AGAIN...

STRIKE

2!

AND THEN ON HIS

3ʳᵈ SWING

HE HIT THE BALL OUT OF

THE PARK!

SPARKY

LOVED TO PLAY CATCH

SO HE RAN
AFTER
THE BALL.

BUT A CAR THAT WAS

RACING DOWN THE STREET

STRUCK

SPARKY.

AND SPARKY

CLOSED HIS

EYES FOREVER.

VICTOR

WAS DEVASTATED.

HE RAN TO THE PET CEMETERY AND

DUG UP SPARKY.

HE INVENTED A SPECIAL MACHINE,

HOOKED UP
SPARKY

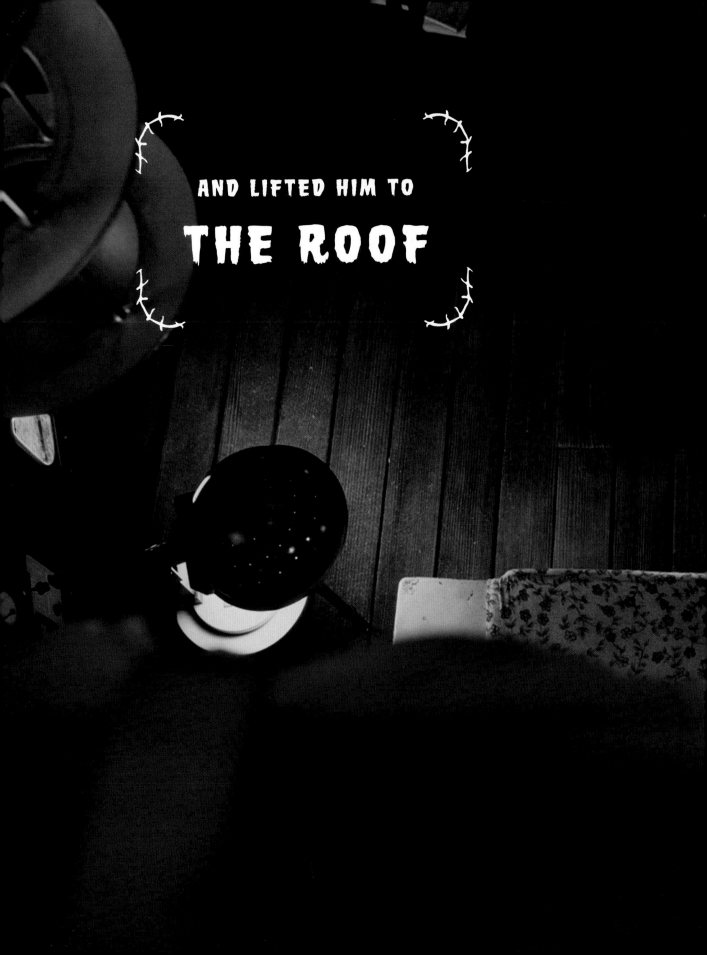

AND LIFTED HIM TO

THE ROOF

A LIGHTNING STORM WAS RAGING
AND IT CRASHED DOWN
ON SPARKY.

WHEN VICTOR LOWERED
DOWN SPARKY HE LOOKED AT
THE DOG AND THOUGHT HE

HAD FAILED

BUT THEN

SPARKY WAGGED HIS TAIL!

ALIVE!

VICTOR WAS SO HAPPY TO HAVE

HIS BEST
FRIEND BACK.

HE TRIED TO KEEP HIM HIDDEN
SO AS NOT TO SCARE
THE NEIGHBORS.

BUT SPARKY ALWAYS MANAGED

TO SNEAK OUT...

AND SOON OTHERS

FOUND OUT

ABOUT SPARKY

AND WANTED TO BRING BACK
THEIR OWN PETS AS WELL.

SOON

THERE WAS A SLEW OF THEM...

NEW HOLLAND WAS TERRORIZED BY A
WERE-RAT...

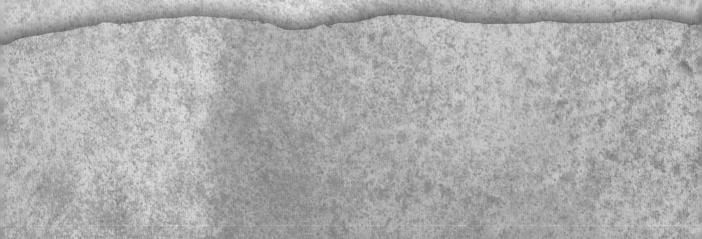

...A
VAMPIRE
CAT...

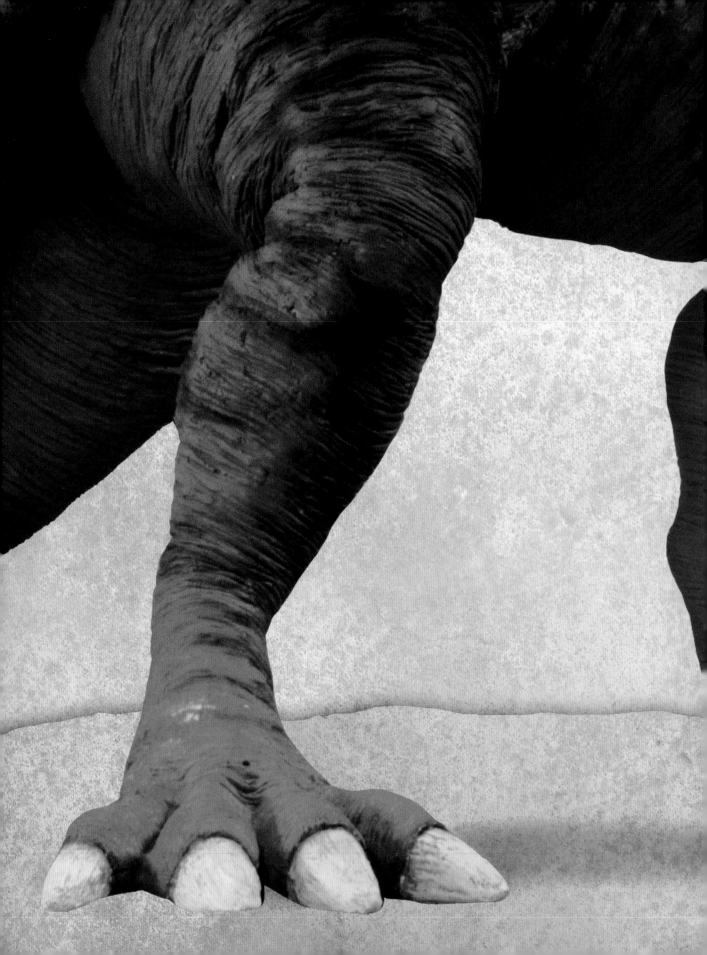

...A TURTLE MONSTER...

...MONSTERS FROM THE SEA,

AND EVEN...

A MUMMY HAMSTER!

...BUT

THERE WOULD

ONLY EVER BE . . .